Children start learning to read long before they start school. They are interested in print wherever it occurs—on posters, food packets, television, in newspapers and books. Story books are a particular source of enjoyment because they provide the opportunity to share make-believe worlds. To start with, children share a story by having it read aloud. Later they are able to take over some of the reading for themselves and eventually they will read simple texts unaided.

In order to do these things, young children need books which have:

- well-matched words and pictures so that they can get the story right when they look at the pictures
- language which they can easily predict and remember
- stories which are satisfying and worthwhile

Ready-to-Read books are designed with all these things in mind. They are ideal for:

- reading aloud to children
- sharing with children
- independent reading by children who have begun to read

All the Ready-to-Read books are suitable for young children, whatever their reading ability, but they have been arranged into three levels to help parents and teachers match the complexity of the text to the reading ability of the child. Level **1** books are the easiest to read, level **3** the most difficult.

This is a level **2** book.

**Educational Consultant:
Cliff Moon, Principal Lecturer,
Bulmershe College, Reading**

D1347680

"NOT NOW!" SAID THE COW

A LITTLE ROOSTER BOOK   0 553 17669 2

First publication in Great Britain

PRINTING HISTORY

Little Rooster edition published 1989

Series graphic design by Alex Jay/Studio J
Associate Editor: Randall Reich

Special thanks to James A. Levine, Betsy Gould, Erin B. Gathrid, and
Whit Stillman.

Little Rooster Books are published by Transworld Publishers Ltd.,
61-63 Uxbridge Road, Ealing, London W5 5SA, in Australia by
Transworld Publishers (Australia) Pty. Ltd., 15-23 Helles Avenue,
Moorebank, NSW 2170, and in New Zealand by Transworld
Publishers (N.Z.) Ltd., Cnr. Moselle and Waipareira Avenues,
Henderson, Auckland.

Made and printed in U.S.A.

Ready-to-Read™

"Not Now!" Said the Cow

by Joanne Oppenheim
Illustrated by Chris Demarest

A Byron Preiss Book

A LITTLE ROOSTER BOOK™

One day a little black crow
spotted a sack of corn seed
lying on the ground.

"Caw, caw!" he crowed.
"Just what we need—
a sack of seed!"

So the little black crow
flew back to the farm.

"Caw, caw!" he crowed.
"Look what I found just lying around.
Who will help me plant
these seeds in the ground?"

"Not now," mooed the cow.

"I'm asleep," baaed the sheep.

"Oh," cawed the crow. "Then I will do it
ALL BY MYSELF."

Soon the sprouts were tall and green,
but weeds were growing in between.

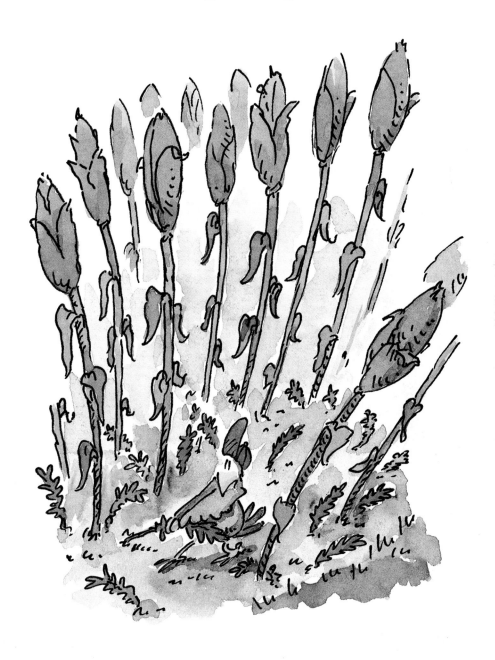

"Who will help me pull the weeds?"

"Fiddlesticks!" peeped the chicks.

"I'm asleep,"
baaed the sheep.

"Not now," mooed the cow.

"Oh," cawed the crow. "Then I will do it
ALL BY MYSELF."

The rows of corn grew tall and thick.
Soon, fat green ears were ready to pick.

"Who will help me pick the corn?"

"Why me?" brayed the donkey.

"Fiddlesticks!" peeped the chicks.

"I'm asleep,"
baaed the sheep.

"Not now,"
mooed the cow.

"Oh," cawed the crow. "Then I will do it
ALL BY MYSELF."

The crow picked the ears one by one,
and late that night his work was done.

"Who will help me thresh the corn?"

"Don't be funny,"
squealed the bunny.

"Why me?"
brayed the donkey.

"Fiddlesticks!"
peeped the chicks.

"I'm asleep,"
baaed the sheep.

"Not now," mooed the cow.

"Oh," cawed the crow. "Then I will do it
ALL BY MYSELF."

Now all that corn was still on the cob, and taking it off was a big, big job.

"Who will help me shell the corn?"

"Not my job,"
grunted the hog.

"Don't be funny,"
squealed the bunny.

"Why me?"
brayed the donkey.

"Fiddlesticks!"
peeped the chicks.

"I'm asleep,"
baaed the sheep.

 "Not now,"
mooed the cow.

"Oh," cawed the crow. "Then I will do it
ALL BY MYSELF."

Then the crow put the corn into a pot.
"What we need," he said,
"is a fire that's hot.

Who will help me gather wood?"

"I can't do that," meowed the cat.

"Not my job," grunted the hog.
"Don't be funny," squealed the bunny.
"Why me?" brayed the donkey.
"Fiddlesticks!" peeped the chicks.
"I'm asleep," baaed the sheep.
"Not now," mooed the cow.

"Oh," cawed the crow. "Then I will do it ALL BY MYSELF."

Soon the wood was burning hot, and the little black crow put a lid on the pot.

"Who will help me shake the pot?"

"I don't dare!" whinnied the mare.

"I can't do that," meowed the cat.
"Not my job," grunted the hog.
"Don't be funny," squealed the bunny.
"Why me?" brayed the donkey.
"Fiddlesticks!" peeped the chicks.
"I'm asleep," baaed the sheep.
"Not now," mooed the cow.

"Oh," cawed the crow. "Then I will do it
ALL BY MYSELF."

So the little black crow
shook the corn in the pot. . . .
He shook it and shook it
til the pot got hot. . . .

And suddenly,
inside that pot,
the corn got hot
and would not stop.
It just kept going. . .

"Where's my share?" whinnied the mare.
"I'll take that!" meowed the cat.
"That's my job," grunted the hog.
"Yummy, yummy,"
squealed the bunny.
"For me! For me!" brayed the donkey.
"First licks," peeped the chicks.
"Let's eat," baaed the sheep.
"Oh, wow!" mooed the cow.

"No, no!" cawed the crow.
"I planted the seeds.
I pulled the weeds.
When the corn was tall,
I picked it all.
I threshed it, shelled it,
and built the fire.
I shook the pot
til it got hot.
And now I'll eat
this nice, hot popcorn. . .

ALL BY MYSELF.''